"The mass of men
lead lives of quiet desperation."
~ Henry David Thoreau

"The cause <u>and cure</u> of discontent,
even desperation, resides inside of every
man, regardless of his station."
~ Mark Fourniér

## Dedication and Acknowledgements

*The Giving Game* was originally written for participants in my empowerment course to describe a game I play with my friends and family. I was first able to test it out on my favorite guinea pig, **Marsha** Fourniér (my very supportive wife); and so, I think it appropriate that I dedicate this book to *her*.

In addition, I owe a tremendous debt of gratitude to others with whom I play *The Giving Game*; and without whom, this book would be a very different animal indeed... perhaps, even one needing to be 'locked up.' So, thanks from the bottom of my heart go to **Patty Kyle, Sherrie Nattrass, Wendy Christensen and Sherolyn Langston**.

Published by

## Fourniér Media

PO Box 83853 Phoenix, AZ 85071-3853
www.CenterForEmpowerment.com

Art Direction: Patricia Kyle

Fourth Edition © Copyright 2003

Fourniér, Inc. All rights reserved. No portion of this document may be copied or transferred in any medium without express written consent of the publisher.

Please visit our web site, www.CenterForEmpowerment.com, and see for yourself the opportunities that exist for taking permanent control of *your* life, and for dramatically impacting your organization.

If you would like to order more of our empowering books (or their audio versions performed on CD to music), feel free to order through our web site or call: 602-997-2422 (toll free 877-770-7788).

# Forward

Joe Iacuzzo, **Universal Pictures**: Editor - Jurassic Park Institute

"This inspirational book is ***Jonathon Livingston Seagull***, ***The Night Before Christmas*** and ***It's a Wonderful Life*** all rolled into one! It would make a great **movie**!"

### Dr. James Nelson
**Editor - *Chicken Soup for the Entrepreneurial Soul*, COO** - The Eagle Institute

"Everyone treasures a handful of very special books, the ones that finally fall apart from reading over and over. If you're looking for another gem that you'll treasure enough to pass on to friends and family, open the cover of Mark Fourniér's, ***The Giving Game***. Be sure you have an uninterrupted thirty minutes. You really won't be able to put it down until you've savored every sparkling facet. I love it! It's too wonderful! I liked the book so well I read it aloud to my 13-year old, who also loved it. I certainly think parents will love reading it to their children."

### Boye Lafayette De Mente
**Founder - Phoenix Books Publishers, President - Arizona Authors Association**,
World Renown Author of over 40 books on Asian culture and philosophy

"Genius Mark Fourniér has done it again, with *The Giving Game*, a gem of a little book that calms, heals and inspires the spirit. A modern day Zen Master, able to distinguish (and teach) 'reality' from 'non-reality,' Mark is also empowering the world through his brilliant insights and programs. He is Dr. Deming, Tom Peters and the Dalai Lama rolled into one! I can't wait to see the next one in his new empowerment series!"

### Dr. Craig Phelps
**Head Physician - Phoenix Suns, Founder - Arizona School of Health Sciences**

"*The Giving Game* takes the reader on a journey faced by each of us: How to successfully navigate the sometimes-treacherous waters of our intimate relationships. [It addresses] the crux of verbal and nonverbal communication, and reveals how each individual's actions determine the success or failure of his/her relationships."

# Introduction

If through this book, I am able to contribute to you in *any* way, I will have fulfilled *my* goal; in which case, *you* will have contributed to *me* as well, for which I thank you. (We refer to this phenomenon in our Empowerment Course of Action as *The Circle of Contribution*).

This book deals with various subjects, including, but not limited to the following: Creating Peace & Harmony, Living in Appreciation, Living in a Continuous State of Contribution and Healing from Loss & Death.

It is my profound hope that you will gain enough inspiration and meaning from this little story to last the whole year through. If, however, by year's end, your life begins to slip or your inspiration dwindles (as inspiration often does), I hope you'll pick up this book and peek through the pages once again. You may be surprised at the new discoveries awaiting every visit.

And, who knows… maybe… just *maybe*, you'll find yourself playing *The Giving Game* as well.

Until then,

**Love more… Laugh more…**
**Live more… Give more.**

Sincerely,

*Mark Fourniér*

# The Giving Game

## A Story

### by Mark Fourniér

Once upon a winter's eve,

between what's real and make believe,

beyond the things we can't conceive…

Playful stars

    danced and darted…

        to the coo of quails

            and nightingales…

above a

humble,

little hovel

on a hill.

Here, a solitary couple
cuddled quietly,
as they huddled
in their hidden, hilltop home.

Though their lives
appeared serene,
things aren't always
as they seem.

'Neath the surface,
they both grieved.
Their sorrow sheathed,
still breathed… and seethed.

There once had been a time

when tenderly they touched,

along the clovered climb

to their happy, homey hutch…

trading tickly, tingly kisses

    that lightly lit upon their lips,

        in eager nips…

            and sips.

A whimsical world
they had shared
with a magical child
who filled the air
with laughter…
and a reverent sense of wonder.

Their love affair with life
nearly never knew of strife.
Their gratefulness
turned everything to gold.

Yet, they slowly took for granted
the blessings they had shared,
till both were disenchanted…
till neither of them cared.

Silently unnoticed,
their vows began to fray,
until their world of wonder
slowly slipped away.

Eventually they settled
for lives of little lies…
doing just enough
to fool prying eyes.

Survival-mode mentality altered their reality, infecting every aspect of their lives.

Instead of living life

in bolting bursts of passion,

they shrugged along indifferently,

existing apathetically…

They muttered… and groaned,

and moped… and moaned,

wasting away…

their lives of gray.

Lackluster lives, however,

cannot go on… forever…

There appears to be a cosmic force

    that keeps us growing on our course,

        making certain

            we move forward

                in our lives…

When life begins to stab and sting

    and stomp on us with everything;

        if nothing else, it forces us to Live!

And when we look at all our gains,

we find that most result from pains…

pains through which…

we benefit and grow.

And, so it was that they were shown

a chance to change the paths they'd sown:

A painful lesson was unclad,

as death barged in… and took their lad.

As shock withdrew,
they thought it through…
and found themselves regretting
all the things they didn't do.

They wished more time
was spent together…
just rolling on the floor.

They thought their chance
would last forever…
Now, forever… was no more.

Nor had either recently

fallen to their knee...

to hold... and kiss...

and love their child,

while crying gratefully.

By taking life for granted,

they now paid the price...

losing what they loved the most,

their unwilling sacrifice.

Doom and gloom now filled the room,
and lingered in a way
that only death can loom.

It ravaged, raped and robbed
their innocence and certainty of life.

There were many others
 suffering on the hill…

The couple's nearby neighbors
 had pains… all just as real.

Everyone, it seemed,
 was merely getting by.
Most had lost their passion…
 some, their will to try.

Their troubles started long before,
but it wasn't till the day…
 they looked…
 for someone
 else to blame
 that evil… came…
their way.
 Surely 'someone' was to blame
for their unhappiness and pain…
the disappointments and misfortunes
 that came…
 and came…
 and came…

Each began to look around
for a culprit to be found.
They looked across the table.
They searched their hilltop town.

They looked for signs of evil;
and doing so they found…
in the hamlet 'neath their burrow,
there was evil all around.

It started when a villager,
from this hamlet down below...

was spotted by the hill folk
walking through their snow.

They hated how he trudged and trekked
across their virgin flecks.
To hill folk, snow was precious…
to be walked on with respect!

By searching hard enough

to find a foe to fault,

the hill folk found the villagers

deserving their assault.

It didn't stop with that...

It never does, you know.

Once we focus on what's wrong,

the list can't help but grow...

The villagers had better land,
more helping hands,
more plows.

Who could help but covet
their plows…
and cows …
and WOWs?

And, it was clearly known,
by nearly everyone,
the village had
bizarre beliefs…
quite frightening…
were some!

The hill folk roared,
"It isn't fair…The villagers won't share.
Some say they even dare to pray
a different kind of prayer."

"They are wrong and we are right,
as anyone can see!
God will help us show them...
We'll force them to agree!"

Self-righteous wars they launched,
and justified the pain...
believing someone had to suffer
for someone else to gain.

And all the while, the *villagers* couldn't get *their* fill…

while wishing from the start *they* could live upon the hill…

"Hill folk have a better view…
They look down on us, we feel.
And, they're so close to God up there,
they barely need to kneel!"

Though both groups felt that greed
was the other's greatest flaw,
they were equally as guilty
of wanting what *they* saw.

"They are wrong and we are right,"
came the villagers' decree,
"God will help us show them…
We'll force them to agree!"


They called each other evil,
and vowed to make things 'right'…
They'd 'fix' their fellow man,
by destroying him with spite!

Each engaged in war,
feeling free of sin...
both sides sure that God
wanted them to win.

It was easier to blame
their troubles on each other.
Instead of looking deep within,
they blamed them on their 'brother.'

They suffered from a lack of love,
a lack of gratitude and sharing.
Perhaps, the greatest lack of all
was that of selfless caring.

One thing was for certain...
Evil did exist...

It
lurked
and lured...
and loathed...
and... hisssssed...
and grew each time
**they raised their fists!**

It fed on hate… It thrived on blame,
but traveled by another name…
for FEAR… was the alias of evil.

They feared there wouldn't
be enough… enough to go around…
They feared that someone else
would take the security they'd found.

Taking this… taking that,
always taking something needed…
They'd take their happiness,
their peace of mind…
the fields that they had seeded.

In the name of keeping others
from taking what was theirs,
they each did the taking…
claiming it was fair.

The more they fought to take
the things they thought they needed,
the more they wound up needing
the things they fought to take.

Some tried not to think about
the war their people waged.

Evil's endless appetite
　had clearly been misgauged,
　　　which now uncaged,
　　　　　raged...
　　　　　　　and raged...
　　　　　　　　　and raged!

"It's not my fault," they uttered,
    if only to themselves,
"I'm not the one who wanted war.
    I wanted something else."

Peace and love had lost their hold…
Brotherhood was turning cold,
and still they strained…
for someone else to blame.

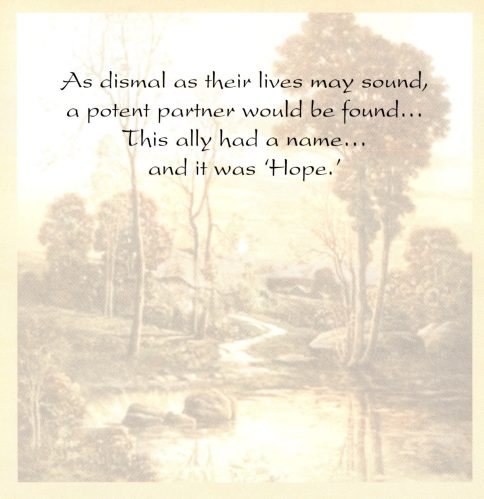

As dismal as their lives may sound,
a potent partner would be found…
This ally had a name…
and it was 'Hope.'

And, one thing

    hope will never do…

        is never… never… ever

            give up on hope.

And, so it was
this winter's eve,
between what's real
and make believe,
beyond the things
we can't conceive…

that stars began to shine so bright
the moon was jealous of their light,
which overflowed to spill…
upon the humble,
little hovel on the hill.

Brightest of the stars that night,
was said by those below the site,
to reach beyond and touch...
this lonely, little, hidden, hilltop home.

Could it be

that good can come,

of even wars

that can't be won,

by somehow

making heroes

of us all?

The youngest hero on this day,
a loving lad from far away,
softly sang as he hiked along the hill.

Black as night, his hair was quite
a contrast to his eyes,
which glowed as bright as diamonds,
like starlight in the skies.

Though he and parents parted,
 his selfless courage started
  when village sisters,
   orphaned too,
    asked the lad
     what they
      should do.

From stinging toes
to sniffling nose,
the little lasses shivered
in the icy evening air.

Their stomachs growled...
as they prowled,
in search of
food to share.

He led the frail and frightened sisters
 gently up the hill
  in search of warmth…
   and shelter…
    and a meal.
While climbing to the hovel
  (starlit bright as day),
   he saw an image in his heart
   of a couple down the way…

The pain he felt inside their souls
seemed greater than his own.
And when he reached the summit,
and peeked inside the home…

he saw them sadly huddled there,
exactly as was shown.

The girls watched him watch them,
as though he'd known them all his life.
He seemed to know the husband's thoughts
and the feelings of the wife.

She was giving up on living…
He could see her life-light dimming,
and knew he must do something…
                    very soon.


She sat beside the hearth
and began to say a prayer,
the kind that desperate people pray
when they have nothing left to share…
and nothing, but their souls…
                    left to bare.

Instead of asking God
to ease her ceaseless pain,
she felt that such a prayer
by now would be in vain.

And, so she said a selfless prayer
for those who would remain.

The loving lad pressed closer
making certain he could hear,
and when she spoke her simple words,
he knew why he was here…

"I ask you Lord
　　for Peace on Earth
　　　　and love to those in need.
Please help them
　　learn of kindness…
　　　　this is what I plead."

Her husband overheard this plea.
He heard her make it selflessly,
then joined in quite excitedly,
believing selfless prayers
are always answered.

The lad drew both the sisters near,
and whispering softly in their ear,
slightly shimmered,
as he slowly shared his plan…
"I know you're cold and hungry,
but there's something we must do…
This clutching couple isn't coping,
and they need some help…
from you."

The girls' hunger was forgot,
while sharing his heroic plot.

They listened closely to the lad,
and the thoughtful thoughts he had,
while his magic plan took flight
that bright, star-blazing night.

Though villagers might not allow
their girls to help hill folk right now,
these little lasses made a vow
to do whatever they could do
(which helped him… help them too).


And, though they'd miss the loving lad
(who smiled like their father had),
they slowly turned…
and tapped…
upon the door.

Having done all he could do that night,
the lad slipped slowly out of sight,
toward the village…
in the valley…
down below.

Their tiny fists
scarce made a sound.
Still these girls
would softly pound,
until their freezing
forms were found…

or till their hands
were just too sore,

to languish longer
on the door.

After what seemed to be
verging on eternity,
the woman they had seen inside...
appeared.

She silently surveyed
dirty prints their feet had made
upon her strictly-sterile
steps of stone.

The little lasses lasted
as long as they could bear,
hoping she would welcome them inside.

Then, pleading they were all alone,
explained they'd lost their only home…

Through war…
their village parents both had died.

The woman helplessly stood still,
staring off atop her hill…
too numb to care
or notice they were there.

Refugees of war,
upon seeing too much gore,
say it all stops seeming real,
until one day… they cannot feel.

So, catatonically they gaze
at even children's open graves...
and carnage few of us
will ever know.

Trapped inside this zone,
the woman turned to stone.
To her, their plea for help
was but a distant drone.

Her husband saw
her standing there.
He understood
her vacant stare…

But, pleas like theirs
were not to go unheeded,
not when help was…
oh so clearly needed.

He felt his heart begin to pound...
Stinging teardrops struck the ground.

He'd found a purpose like before...
    before death knocked,
        before the war,
            before all this...
                and so much more.

He swept the little girls up into his arms,
then very gently lowered them inside.

They did not resemble
 the pain he'd seen before.

This time it wasn't death
 knocking at the door.

Already he was healing…
 His soul grew warm with feeling.
 As he hugged and held them tightly,
 his spirits lifted slightly.

And, in that magic moment,
he became aware…
his pain began to vanish…
when he began to care.

He saw his future suddenly
change to one of joy,
by learning from the loss
of his precious little boy.

The husband told his listless wife,
"It's time that we get on with life.
We need to put away the past...
stop mourning for what's missing
from our lives.

Let's focus on the beauty still,
surrounding us atop our hill.
Our life is what we choose to see.
We decide what it will be."

She blankly stared across at him.
She wasn't ready to give in…
There were still so many crosses…
left to bear.

And so his lost, lamenting wife
shuffled off resenting life.
She couldn't love… She couldn't give.
She couldn't see the point to live.

As he blew out all the candles,
and closed the shutters for the night,
her husband came across
a most peculiar sight.
It sat upon the mantle,
above the firelight…

It was just a little card,
nothing much at all.
It wasn't written
by his wife,
and the girls
were much too small…
But, here it lay
upon the mantel just the same

*The Giving Game*

He could tell the card was rare,
so he opened it with care...
then slowly read the lyrical lines aloud:

### The Giving Game

Whatever we harbor within our hearts
is the harbor in which we live,
for the pain or blessings we receive
are reflections of those we give.


Kindness, compassion, laughter and love
are gifts I give to you.
And, as you pass these gifts along,
you'll find they bless you too.

On back of this card was a bonus...
the secret to peace on earth!

He trembled as he read
and understood its worth:

*The 'Peace on Earth,'
of which men speak,
begins with 'peace at home.'
When we learn to love our own lives,
peace...will happen on its own.*

Vexed and perplexed,
   he glanced around,
      hoping to find
         what couldn't be found…
            not a hint or a glint,
               or a sign or a sound…
                  Not even a scent
                     was left for his hound.
                     Whoever had been there
                  left nothing behind…
               nothing… that is…
            that he could find,
         except this one,
      very unusual,
   little card.

He read the mysterious words again,

hoping to make more sense of them.

He rolled the rhymes around

in profound, prophetic ways.

He drank them in

and thought them through,

until the break of day.

He must have drifted off that night,
for he awakened with a keen insight.
And now, he knew just what to do
to turn their lives around:

Reflecting upon an earlier time,
regarding the past for which he pined,
the memories that he'd resigned
flashed and flickered in his mind.
He recalled the life he had before...
before leaving it behind.

His future had held such promise…
   His youth was filled with dreams.


His legendary kindness
   was known to reach extremes.

Kind compassion was his key,
   giving it unselfishly…
giving things he thought he ought…
   giving… just to give.

Some had thought him wealthy…
Others thought him poor…

Whichever way he saw himself
was the version that he bore.

But, he began to fear…

that some had more than he,

or what they had was better;

that's how it seemed to be…

a bigger house (without a mouse),

a nicer wife than he…

a better job, more shish kebab,

a less arthritic knee,

taller trees, smaller fleas…

It went on endlessly.

Soon, he wanted more himself,
which can sometimes be sad.

The more he looked
 for something else,
  the less he saw
   of what he had.

While cursing out his bad knee,
he forgot that one was good.
He was seeing what he couldn't,
while ignoring what he could.

He wanted more and more
and soon became obsessed.
Then, it wasn't just for 'better'…
It had to be the best.

When it comes to those possessions
 that we get… to get… ahead;
 when we have… to have them,
we become… possessed… instead.

He began resenting anything
distracting from his quest.
This soon included wife and son,
his health, his play…　　his rest.

The more he focused on his needs,
the more his wife did hers.
And so, their lives spun 'round in greed,
as discontented blurs.

This poignant, paradox of power
spiraled downward by the hour,
till they both became but obstacles
 to get around each day.

It happened oh so gradually,
 they didn't even see:
 Along this path,
 the dreams they'd shared
 would die... eventually.

But, now he knew he'd found a way
to reverse their destiny,
beginning with the simple task
of living gratefully.

He listed everything he loved
about his house upon the hill.
When compared to those less fortunate,
his life looked better still!

He loved his home!
    He loved his wife!
        He loved his job!
            He loved his life!

Rather than competing
    for the largest house in town,
        he now wanted beating…
            the biggest heart around!

The insight he had gained that night
grew quickly in the morning light.
It formed into an inkling…
then an image… then… a plan.

Business folk and parents
would benefit the same,
when they and those around them
agreed to play this 'game.'

Relationships in every form
would have so much to gain.
No matter what the storms in life,
they'd see beyond the rain.

"Pass these gifts along," it said,
upon the card from which he'd read.

And so, he joined 'The Giving Game,'
a game that all could win…
while learning that their happiness
comes only from within.

When this hyper-helpful husband
figured out the rules,
he gave them out as gifts…
He thought of them as jewels.

He gave them to his customers,
then served instead of sold.
He filled their needs so selflessly,
they offered him their gold.

The gold they gave was trust,
and friends they sent his way,
knowing he would treat *them*
in the same unselfish way.

He took a chance his wife would play
and started with a kiss…

the first that they had shared
since their child was amiss.

She made a feeble effort,
but her heart was like a sieve.
She couldn't play The Giving Game.
There was nothing left to give.

Re-missing, then dismissing him,
she mumbled soft and low,

"I think this game is senseless.
Just take the girls and go.
No game can stop my heartache now,
no game of which I know."

Her husband kept on playing.
He knew the game was good.

He played with those who wouldn't…
He played with those who would.

By morning it had spread
like fire in a mill,
and the boomerang of kindness
rained love upon the hill.

In just a day, his life had changed,
because his heart was re-arranged…

He'd found the joy of living
he'd lost so long ago,
and he found himself forgiving
the hamlet down below.

Sending down the book of rules
to the village he once blamed,
he asked for their forgiveness…
then offered them his game.

When his wife heard what he'd done,
she prattled and rattled and roared,
"They took away our only son...
Now, you give them a reward!

It isn't fair for you to care,
or treat their orphans like our son,
after all the pain they've caused
and all the wrong they've done!"

Her husband took her in his arms
and kissed her tenderly.

"I understand the way you feel...
That's how I used to be,
until I viewed the other side
and saw how they saw me.

I'm the one who let our son
beat the drum that day,
and lead us into battle,
sure 'God would pave our way.'

Perhaps the village
lost some lads
by thinking
just as I…

that God would
choose one side to live
and let the others… die.

It was not the hand of God,
nor the enemies we bleed.
If anything we bought our pain
through foolish fear and greed.

So, who are we to judge them?
Do we know their plight?
And, are we always perfect?
Do we… always… do what's right?

I'm sure those in the village
do what's right for them…
what's taught by all their parents
to all their 'little men.'

But, I was taught that giving

and kindness would prevail.

I did so in my younger days,

and proved the theory well.

Yet, with all
my giving,
I kept on
getting more.
I couldn't
always
measure it...
I wasn't
keeping
score,
but in the end...
I ended up
more happy
than before.

I'm sure you'll play this game
when I prove it works, my love.
I'll return when I discover how;
till then, farewell my dove."


He asked the little lasses,
"Keep giving to my wife.
Be kind to her, no matter what,
and you'll win this game of life."

They already knew exactly what to do;
   so, off they wooed him…
               off they shooed him…
               off to do…
                    what he
                           must too.

With that, he left his humble home
   and marched off down the hill…
      Driving deep into the darkness,
         he braved the winter chill.

Before too long his wife would see…
      she was needed desperately…

It seemed these frail
   and frightened girls
      were suddenly a mess.
They couldn't
   keep from crying…
      They couldn't even dress!

And then these suffering sisters
suddenly got sick…
They needed help around the clock.
Their tocks would barely tick!

So she fed the little girls…
made sure they said their prayers…
gave comfort through the night…
washed and combed their hair.

She tried to keep from playing
that wretched 'Giving Game,'
but someone had to care for them
and no one else remained.

Still, she wouldn't hold them
or let them get too close…
resenting them as 'villagers'
or fearing love…or both.


When her husband did return,
she'd become aware…
that something stirred inside of her,
though she still tried not to care.

As if by spell, the girls got well

and both began to gleam.

Her husband's face was glowing too,

when he told her what he'd seen:

"By now, you know 'The Giving Game'
    has made it to the sea.
The villagers you've learned to hate
    are playing it with me.

They have many children
    who've lost their moms and dads,
like these sweet-faced lasses…
    and our loving lad.

Of these lads... one they say
appears when stars are bright...
bringing little children
in the middle of the night,
yet leaves no tracks upon the snow,
as he disappears from sight.

They say that he's an angel,
inspired by a tear.
He says (when asked who sent him),
"My mother brought me here...

It happened when she bowed one night
and prayed before the firelight.
She made a plea for peace on earth
and love to those in need…

She asked they learn of kindness,
so this became my creed.

I have come to combat evil,
but peace cannot begin…
not until the peace we seek
is found at first within.

Security and happiness
are purely 'state of mind'…
Looking for them elsewhere
brings emptiness… you'll find.

So, I share with those who care…
both 'peace' and 'peace of mind'
result from 'grateful giving'
and always being kind."

Her husband added sweetly
to the story he'd begun,
a description of this angel…
who looked just like their son.

"He taught that blaming others
fans on evil's flame.
We must BE the answer,
instead of laying blame.

Evil may be with us…
always… everywhere,
but it cannot find a place to grow
when we love…
       and give…
             and care.

We thought we could defeat it
with aggression, blame and hate…
but all that did was feed it,
which brought about our fate.

The only way I know to end
our evil rival's reign…
is to live our lives in gratitude,
and play 'The Giving Game.'



I know the girls we've taken in
don't replicate the joy,
that we once took for granted
when we had our little boy…

If the angel they described to me
 is the son we lost so recently,
perhaps each aching heart we heal
 reminds us…that he's with us still.

And maybe with that prayer you made,
you began… the plans I've laid.
Perhaps the game began with you…
Perhaps you helped create it too.

Remember how you prayed that night
for love to those in need?
Surely these sweet girls deserve
the love for which you plead,
and so my darling wife… do you…



Please tell me you concede."

As she pictured peaceful people.
in the village down below,
and how they'd surely suffered
in ways she'd never know,
a choir began to sing...
they were coming up the hill...

She saw outside her window,
as she leaned against the sill,
a trail of golden torches
lighting lads with little drums,
who led a line of villagers,
bringing flowers…for her son.

No heart of stone, or hardwood door,
could keep out this much love.
Her humble hovel
glowed once more
from starlight
up above...

Then drawing in a long, deep breath,
her hatred died... a silent death.

Her husband played
'The Giving Game'
so well with her
she knew,
that trying
to 'out give'
this gift
was more
than she
could
do.

And then, there were the girls
	standing quietly aside…


What was it he was thinking…
when he carried them inside?

Looking at their faces,
   these lasses torn apart,
sent gushing tears of gratitude
	rushing… to her heart…
which nourished it and softened it…
				at last.

Compelled by sheer compassion,
she fell upon her knee,
and held... and kissed...
and loved them,
while crying gratefully.
And, they returned
the love that grew...
times two.

The Circle
   of Contribution...
      was complete.

Who won The Giving Game that day?
Whose 'grateful giving' set them free?
No matter who was asked, they'd say,
"The Giving Game was won… by ME!"

# Epilogue

As you may imagine,
the hill folk made amends.
They asked their village neighbors
to see them as their friends.


But over time this epic…
became a fairy tale.
The Giving Game was long forgot…
its lessons were as well…

Yet, now we have a chance it seems
to re-ignite these hopeful dreams,
while making efforts every day
to play The Giving Game some way.

We plant a magic seed each time
we live the lessons of this rhyme.
Thus with every seed unfurled,
we'll each have grown… a better world.

Comments from those who've played the Giving Game:

"After our children moved away, my husband and I settled into lives of 'quiet desperation.' However, when we began to play *The Giving Game*, we again discovered the joy of giving to each other like we did when we were dating. As a matter of fact, my husband contributes more to me now than he ever did. Because of his little acts of giving, I find myself wanting to give more too. What fun it is to try thinking of ways to contribute and then seeing the happiness that simple act creates. I now know that *The Giving Game* is the game of life. How can I not play it with everyone I know?" ~ Patricia Kyle

"I've discovered that using *The Giving Game* in a corporate environment promotes increased integrity and fairness. I also believe that increased customer satisfaction is an additional benefit of playing this wonderful game!" ~ Thomas Rudeen, Boeing.

"Playing *The Giving Game* is contagious! I have begun performing unexpected acts of kindness that, before this book, went as unfulfilled good intentions. I play it in big and small ways and watch as magical changes take place in my life, both inside and out. How grateful I am for a book that teaches not only me, but my children and grandchildren, the power of contributing to others!" ~ Sherrie Nattrass

"*The Giving Game* is a delightful, feel-good book. In my experience, when the principles taught by Mr. Fourniér are followed, positive improvements result in relationships, depression, co-dependency and self-esteem. I highly recommend not only reading *The Giving Game*, but playing it too!"
~ Robert E. Stahn, Licensed Mental Health and Marriage Counselor

"I continually experiment with variations of *The Giving Game*. Recently I asked my wife to share her greatest needs and priorities with me. I then merged them with my own, as if they were MY priorities as well. I am contributing to her more profoundly than ever before, because I am now doing the things that *she* says matter. In response, she has been more tolerant, appreciative and supportive of me than she has ever been." ~ Mark Fourniér

# Appendix

This tiny tale was written to offer insight and inspiration; but more importantly, to provide the reader with an opportunity to LIVE the principles featured herein, by actually PLAYING The Giving Game in his or her real life. Because living in a state of appreciation (thanks) and contribution to others (giving) are the most important elements of *The Giving Game*, you might consider reinforcing these lessons by sharing this tale with loved ones at Christmas or Thanksgiving time each year.

*Below are the rules to play this game… Your life will never … be the same.*

## The Giving Game rules:

★ Start off with a list of what you *love* and *appreciate* about your life (humbly keeping in mind that there are *always* others *less* fortunate than you).

★ Select a beneficiary and *selflessly* contribute to that person or group every chance you get… with no expectation of *reward* or *appreciation* for your efforts. Attempt to make *their* priorities *yours*. You might even choose to do it *anonymously* and leave behind a little 'Giving Game' card of your *own*. (ANY selfless acts, words or deeds of kindness are considered as 'contributions').

★ Create a list of what you love and/or appreciate about the person or group to whom you are contributing. Focus on that list. If possible, *share* it with him/her/them.

★ It is possible to *compete* with someone by attempting to out-contribute him or her. In this case, once one of you has made so *many* contributions (or a contribution of such magnitude that the other is unable to surpass it), he or she appreciatively concedes the victory to the *contributing* challenger, and the game is officially started over from the beginning (It is possible to declare a *tie*). Either way, *everyone always* wins!

Author, Mark Fourniér

# About the Author

Founder of The Center for Empowerment and creator of its life-altering courses, **Mark** also writes produces and directs television programming where he has won over 80 national and international awards including: three EMMY Awards, the Cable Ace Award, First Place at the US/International Film Festival and the National Vision Award for his innovative concepts in the field of human development

Featured on Dateline NBC, Comedy Central and in the upcoming book, *Chicken Soup for the Entrepreneurial Soul*, his empowering programs have been broadcast on all major networks.

Mark is also a multi-patent inventor and the author of eight entertaining and inspiring books in the field of human behavior and performance, as well as the head of Eepiphany Entertainment, an 'inspirational' book publishing and record label company.

He and his family reside in both Chicago, Illinois and Paradise Valley, Arizona, where he is first and foremost a committed husband and father.